VISIONARY TRIBUTES

"The resonance I feel with Damanhur and the mission of The Oracle Institute fills me with passionate promise for the future of the human race. Coherence of this magnitude is a clear indication of a deep pattern within the universe, and it is the same force which guides my work at the Foundation for Conscious Evolution, The Shift Network, and with colleagues throughout the world."

~ **Barbara Marx Hubbard,** co-founder of the Foundation for Conscious Evolution; global ambassador for The Shift Network; member of the Evolutionary Leaders Group, World Future Society, and Assoc. for Global New Thought; and author of *The Hunger of Eve, Emergence: The Shift from Ego to Essence,* and *Birth 2012 and Beyond*

"The Damanhur community is a truly paradigm-expanding experiment in conscious living. Its design, evolution, and artistry are a testament to the unique genius of Falco – an evolutionary pioneer."

~ **Stephen Dinan, M.A.,** founder and CEO of The Shift Network; member of the Evolutionary Leaders Group; and author of *Radical Shift: Spiritual Writings from the Voices of Tomorrow* and *Sacred America: Fulfilling Our Country's Promise* with Marianne Williamson

"Here is the revelation of the soul of a mystery school, that once and future experience of exploring the ways in which the self is put into service for the SELF ... and the world mind grows as a consequence."

~ **Jean Houston, Ph.D.,** founder of The Foundation for Mind Research, Renaissance of Spirit Mystery School, and the Jean Houston Foundation for social artistry; global advisor on human development to the United Nations and UNICEF; and author of *A Passion for the Possible, A Mythic Life,* and *The Wizard of Us*

"These books are a poetic tribute to the Absolute bearing witness to its own creation through the eyes of a deeply inspired mystic."

~ **Andrew Cohen,** spiritual teacher and founder of EnlightenNext; and author of *My Master Is My Self, Embracing Heaven & Earth,* and *Evolutionary Enlightenment* with Deepak Chopra

"History hinges on the lives and actions of great individuals. Building the Temples of Humankind was a mission from a higher spiritual world. Falco has inspired a community to bring heaven to earth."

~ **Alex Grey and Allyson Grey, M.F.A,** founders of the Chapel of Sacred Mirrors (CoSM), a sanctuary for encouraging the creative spirit; publishers of *Damanhur: Temples of Humankind;* and Alex is Chair of the Sacred Art Department at Wisdom University and author of *Sacred Mirrors, The Mission of Art,* and *Net of Being*

"Falco is an explorer at the frontiers of the human experience. He sees what others only intuit, and he thereby provides insight into the potential for the human future in that domain of our identity where there are at present deep yearnings but no maps."

~ **Jim Garrison, Ph.D.,** founder and CEO of Ubiquity University; founder of Wisdom University and The State of the World Forum; and author of *America As Empire, Civilization and The Transformation of Power,* and *Climate Change and the Primordial Mind*

"This look into the personal perspectives of Falco – a living Avatar – is a poetic walk through the internal work and wisdom of one who has brought us astonishing beauty and creativity. You'll find practical wisdom interwoven with cosmic musings that result in a provocative and enlightening window into the mind of a very special man."

~ **John L. Petersen,** futurist and founder of The Arlington Institute; author of *A Vision for 2012: Planning for Extraordinary Change* and *Out of the Blue: How to Anticipate Big Future Surprises;* and publisher of the e-newsletter *FUTUREdition*

"The *Three Books of the Initiate* are uniquely different than any other spiritual books on the market today – and I do mean unique. They read as if Oberto were interpreting my third near-death experience, seeing what I saw, feeling what I felt, lending heft to that sense of Presence when you truly become one with The One. The texts stretch thought about who we are, where we came from, and why we're here. The books are stunningly powerful."

~ **P.M.H. Atwater, L.H.D.,** researcher of near-death and evolutionary states; and author of *The Real Truth About Death, Children of the Fifth World, Beyond the Indigo Children, Future Memory,* and *Near-Death Experiences: The Rest of the Story*

"What appeals to me about Falco's exposition is that the perspective on learning and growing into the light is one of personal responsibility, with apparently no absolutes. Like Edgar Cayce's practical philosophy, it assumes each person is capable of achieving self-realization. Thanks for making this book available in English."

> ~ **Henry Reed, Ph.D.,** Director of the Edgar Cayce Institute for Intuitive Studies; professor at Atlantic University; founder of Creative Spirit Studios; and author of *Dream Medicine, Dream Solutions, Awakening Your Psychic Powers,* and *Sharing Your Intuitive Heart*

"The *Three Books of the Initiate* are a love poem to humanity, written by a man drunk with the Divine. They are a wakeup call, inviting each of us to let go of what is no longer serving us and to learn how to behave. They are an invitation to embrace the Source that is manifesting through each of us and everything, and that is patiently waiting for us to remember who we truly are."

> ~ **Philip Hellmich,** Director of Peace at The Shift Network; advisor to the Global Peace Initiative of Women; co-author of *The Love: Of the Fifth Spiritual Paradigm* (Oracle Institute Press); and author of *God and Conflict* with Lama Surya Das

"Reading Falco's inspiring books feels like dancing with the Divine. The ego wants to find the logic, but through story and metaphor, the jewels of wisdom land deeply within the soul, resulting in profoundly effortless understanding and illumination."

> ~ **Olivia Parr-Rud, M.S.,** thought-leader and liaison between the spiritual and corporate worlds; and best-selling author of *Data Mining Cookbook* and *Business Intelligence Success Factors: Tools for Aligning Your Business in the Global Economy*

"The *Initiate* series reads like an epic poem. The nature of the Cosmos unfolds throughout these passages, along with the truth of the divine relationship between God and the creatures of Earth. For those who are ready to hear, many mysteries are revealed through the Master's midnight conversations, his secret thoughts, and his guiding hand offered to the Initiates."

> ~ **High Malku Priest Robert Martin, Jr., Ph.D.,** Patriarch of the Ancient and Sovereign Order of Melchizedek; and author of *The Tree of Life Bears Twelve Manner of Fruit: An Alchemical Story*

REBORN TO LIVE

Second Book of the Initiate

OBERTO *"Falco"* AIRAUDI

WITH A FOREWORD BY
ALEX AND ALLYSON GREY

Translated by Elaine Baxendale and
Silvia *"Esperide Ananas"* Buffagni
Edited by Laura M. George

Published by The Oracle Institute Press, LLC

A division of The Oracle Institute, a 501(c)(3) educational charity
1990 Battlefield Drive
Independence, Virginia 24348
www.TheOracleInstitute.org

Copyright © 2013 by Oberto Airaudi
Revised English Edition

Publisher's Cataloging-in-Publication Data

Airaudi, Oberto.
   Reborn to live / Oberto "Falco" Airaudi ; with a foreword by Alex and Allyson Grey ; translated by Elaine Baxendale and Silvia "Esperide Ananas" Buffagni ; edited by Laura M. George. -- Rev. English ed.
   p. cm. -- (Second book of the Initiate)
   LCCN 2013934830
   ISBN 978-1-937465-05-6

   1. End of the world--Fiction. 2. Messiah--Fiction. 3. Human-alien encounters--Fiction. 4. Science fiction. I. Baxendale, Elaine. II. Ananas, Esperide. III. Title. IV. Series: Airaudi, Oberto. Initiate ; 2nd bk.

PS3601.I78R43 2013   813'.6
                                              QBI13-676

Cover and book design by Donna Montgomery
Printed in the United States

CONTENTS

FOREWORD

Alex and Allyson Grey

History hinges on the lives and actions of great individuals. Building the Temples of Humankind at Damanhur was a mission from a higher spiritual world. Oberto "Falco" Airaudi inspired a community to bring heaven to earth. His vision of an underground temple complex captivated the imaginations of a community of artists and artisans, who gathered around him to realize his prophetic vision.

This powerful sharing of a revelation founded a great people – the Damanhurians – with their own constitution, their own money, school, stores, restaurants, galleries, rituals and ceremonies. And then there are the Temples, which every Damanhurian works on in their own way.

Perhaps in a past life, Falco was Horus himself, now returned to liberate the world. Living according to his own vision, individualistic, an attractor, a visionary artist and spiritual leader, Falco inspires our admiration and awe, and he activates our highest intentions as artists and community builders. People have rearranged their lives to gather and create around him.

In preparation for our book *Damanhur: Temples of Humankind* (published by CoSM Press, 2006), we had several occasions to visit the Temples and the Damanhur community. Sacred space initiates people into a body of wisdom. A journey through Damanhur's temple spaces mirrors an alchemical transformation and refinement of the soul. Through the secret temple doors, into the mountain, through curving corridors and connecting rooms, we imagined being digested by the organs of a Deity.

Allyson, Falco, Esperide Ananas, Alex

To motivate and develop a sense of "coopetition" in the community, Falco devised "art wars" that inspired the genesis of outdoor sculptural grounds at Damanhur, each group out-beautifying the other. Additionally, every exquisite hall of the Temples of Humankind is uniquely painted, sculpted, filled with stained glass, and covered with a treasure of mosaic created by the artist community.

The Hall of Water, outstanding among all the Temples of Humankind, is the precious room designed entirely by one mind: Falco. He is an alchemist, working with energies, with force fields around the earth that connect us to the stars. This is the portal that Falco opens with his work, calling us toward a creative engagement with the Celestial Order.

The Book of the Initiate, in its three parts, covers the journey of one whose mind and spirit encompass multiple times and multiple beings. It's the embedded intelligence of the universe coming through the voice of a spiritual hero. This journey of visionary dimensions awakens us by putting us in the mind of an Enlightened Being. Damanhur is a mystery school, and this mythic story is foundational to the Damanhurian tale of the universal Initiate – who we all are.

In an earlier century, Zarathustra was celebrated by Friedrich Nietzsche and God was declared "dead." Today Falco's mythic trilogy hearkens to the aliveness of Spirit in each of us, and the drive to build antennae to the higher dimensions of world teachers and cosmic cousins. The books beckon us to evolve as a species, embrace the diversity of the human religious quest, and recognize our common unity as world citizens. As a result, the texts also inspire us to honor and save the precious lifeweb.

The message we receive from Falco – a mystic artist and storyteller for our times – is that the path of science, creativity and spirituality, united, can form the alchemical incubator needed for a sustainable relationship with nature and a future for the human species. Damanhur, the *Initiate* trilogy, and the many other works of Falco stand as a lighthouse of hope and higher possibility as we navigate the stormy seas of the 21st Century.

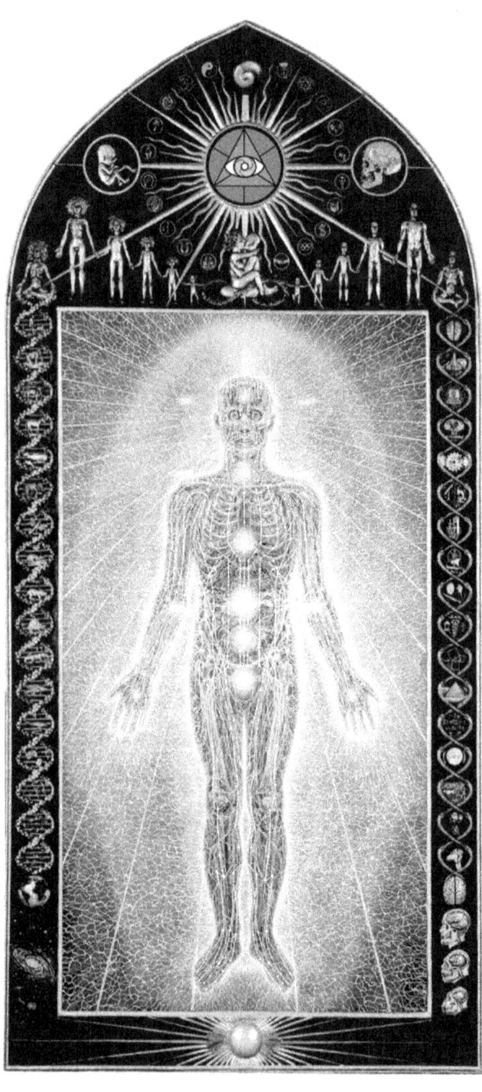

"The Chapel of Sacred Mirrors will bring you face to face with your soul and move you to a new level of Enlightenment."

~ Deepak Chopra

Alex and Allyson Grey

Alex and Allyson Grey are world-renowned artists and co-founders of the Chapel of Sacred Mirrors in New York (CoSM), a sanctuary for contemplation and encouraging the creative spirit. Alex's twenty-one lifesized paintings – the "Sacred Mirrors" – take the viewer on a journey toward their own divine nature by examining the body, mind, and spirit. Begun in 1979, the series took ten years to complete, during which Alex perfected "x-ray" depictions of the human body that reveal the interplay of anatomical and spiritual forces. Alex is Chair of the Sacred Art Department at Wisdom University, and his art has been exhibited at numerous galleries throughout the world.

Alex and Allyson Grey are international art instructors, performance artists, and speakers. At CoSM, the couple teaches MAGI workshops (Mystic Artists Guild International). The Watkins Review named Alex one of the top twenty spiritual leaders alive today, and the Temple of Understanding named Alex and Allyson two of the world's top fifty Interfaith Leaders. The Greys also are sculptors, jewelry designers, and authors and publishers of best-selling books and DVDs, including: *Sacred Mirrors: The Visionary Art of Alex Grey*; *The Mission of Art*; *Art Psalms*; *Damanhur: Temples of Humankind*; and *Net of Being*.

Currently, the Greys are building a new art sanctuary in Wappinger Falls, New York, called "Entheon," which means a "place to discover the God within." The architecture of Entheon points to the transcendent unity of all religions, as depicted by a continuous band of identical Gods which clad the structure. Like tears of mercy, angels fall from the all-seeing eyes of the many-faced Godhead, bridging the realms of humanity and divinity.

www.CoSM.org

PREAMBLE

*I*s the hermit Monk Vadusfadam a sensitive being with subtle mental antennae or a madman who picks up the ideas of the world by listening to the race minds?

A wise man? An Envoy?

An Enlightened One?

Since he was young, Vadusfadam has been a follower of OroCritshna – the Envoy with MEMORY. [1] *OroCritshna used to sit by the fire and talk of what everyone knows deep down inside.*

---

[1] OroCritshna, whom we encountered in *Dying to Learn: First Book of the Initiate*, is he who remembers and who teaches. Vadusfadam, another symbolic name-frequency, represents the Initiate who attains completion of self.

One day Vadusfadam had the opportunity, through the Game of Life, to choose what to do with his existence.[2] He offered all of himself to his Master, to LIFE.

With Indifference, he freely pushed the button and took upon himself the karma that came from it without expecting anything at all in exchange, instead turning down all possible recompense. He offered his body's pain to save the life of whoever was the target of the magical trigger.

Thus, with a profound awareness of his choice, Vadusfadam decided to become Enlightened whenever his teacher OroCritshna might so decide and permit ... without time limits ... without promises of any kind!
Vadusfadam consistently kept to his given word, taking on the pain without hesitation. And by doing so, he moved many steps ahead on the path to realization.

This is the diary of Vadusfadam, the written tale of that solitary man who still remembers the world and its ephemeral ages.

---

[2] Since 1983, the "Game of Life" has been one of Damanhur's social and spiritual paths. Falco wrote *Reborn to Live* during the years of the *viaggio* (journeys), the itinerant phase of the Game of Life, and the book draws images and emtions from that extraordinary experience. It was then possible to attain Enlightenment by solving *koans* (riddles) that were proposed by Falco. Today, the Game of Life continues to support experimentation and innovation within the context of communal projects, such as the "New Life Project" – the latest initiative for facilitating the arrival in Damanhur of people from all over the world, whether for a three month visit or as future residents.

The narrator Alfo and the poet Zela also help us to contact the inner self, open the soul, and hear the voice that resonates within.

Who knows?
Perhaps by following their ideas, lessons, instructions, ordinary words, YOU may be able to find the key, the trigger inside yourself, the combination to unlock the Door and access the treasures stored deep within.

Enjoy the Game!

PART ONE: REBIRTH
Chronicles of a Mad Monk

Times and resurrections. Temples rebuilt, rescued from hard rocks. Even if I do not have a body now, I am here.

The day alternates with rhythmical nights ever faster, and a divine curtain shows me and hides, shows me and hides again the shining sun. But what is the mystery, beyond the veil of words?

In one day the thoughts are many, Alfo. You who wander through human thoughts, you know, tell me. How many times do you change paths, deviating from stagnant puddles?

Zela, do not judge them so. You are too distant from them to see their single lights, to swim in the denseness, in the fire, in the airy liquid cloud that is their sole inner world.

The moment draws upon every message of the world: a flight, a branch, a snowflake on one's nose. Why limit something that has no boundaries, why constrain air in a closed fist, air, which is free and far from form?

My hands now sketch an ancestral rhythm, carving it piece after piece from this drum.
Just one, it has 666 different voices.

You will go mad first. Laughing, you will go mad and you will come to your senses again, behind the curtain, for as long as I want.
Rhyme, rhyme, long and tight, silly and wide ...

The measures of all things are contained in us, Alfo. Why do you persist in watching those tiny crumbs of Time?

The newspaper carries the same words in a different order, and the concepts cross over and endlessly repeat; new words for things even more ancient than our race: fear, rage, pleasure, love, hunger, sleep ...
And everyone's glances and their bodies' secret gestures always tell the same stories, colored by words that are appearance.

"Good morning." (I'd like to pounce on you.)
"Oh, how are you?" (I'm feeling uncomfortable. I'll defend myself.)
"Pretty well, thank you. And you?" (I want you. I've been looking for you. I've been wanting to tell you for so long – that's why I'm aggressive. Don't be afraid of me.)

"Not bad. What's happening with you?" (I've gathered you want me; you've already told me. I've fantasized about it but I need time. I'm not indifferent to you.)

Fade-out: The words fade away and are just a rather distant, useless humming, while the gestures shamelessly tell of a thousand fantasies, free mindedly.

This in each moment, beyond the languages of the world, among odors, winking, colors, movements. Even those who have always been shy and silent have never stopped talking with everyone.

Clouds of ice thick as flocks of bloodthirsty doves eat away at living things. Mists hide and give ephemeral consistency to immense creatures, whose intentions escape me. Snowflakes majestic as planets fall, swimming, to the bottom of the world.

Odin, up in the North once again, creates man from the ash tree and woman from the elm.[3]

Sitting among the mountains, I watch all this, sighing.

The wind from my lips whirls crazily among the man-trees, seemingly far from one another but clinging by the roots, underground. Times and resurrections ...

Mother Frigg cries for her son Balder, killed by his brother Loki. We know he will rise again.[4]

Isis cries for Horus.[5]

---

[3] In Norse mythology, Odin is a god of war, wisdom, magic, and death. He is the ruler of Asgard and the father of Thor.
[4] Frigg is Odin's wife, Queen of Asgard, and goddess of love.
[5] Isis is an Egyptian goddess who miraculously gives birth to her son Horus after her husband Osiris is killed by his brother Set.

With the arrow of poisoned mistletoe, the Winter Lord does not defeat the Unvanquished Sun.

I have waited several millennia to reply to you, Zela. The deaths and rebirths of these creatures are part of us, you see. They become young again in time. We – static, eternal and invincible, without pain, present at everything – we are less free than they. Time, in which they are immersed, makes them suffer, but free.

Boxes of nothing contain infinite realities – among these, a few words stand out, sovereign.

The journey is always long, from home to work. The car races off fast and obedient, swallowing up the tarmac and drawing the world toward it.

On a planet shaped as a sphere you are always going up or going down, depending on how you see things, on where you put the world, above or below.

More than a train or bus driver, I am a ferryman: I carry souls beyond the Styx, to new, fresh pastures and dazzling beaches.[6]

To take in new realities with one's mind is part of the play of crystals. To play between one breath and another gives an electrifying sense of everything stopping. Then, to your amazement – everything immobile around you, gestures in mid-air – you walk wandering through the streets, where cars drive by unmoving, breaths are stilled, and pigeons remain suspended in the void.

---

[6] In Greek mythology, the Styx is a river that separates Earth from Hades.

Why me, world? Am I too fast, or have you stopped?

You can rummage in people's pockets, enter everywhere. Nobody will stop you. You can caress, touch, take. Nobody will know.

When you are tired, the world will begin its beat again and you can swim in time, once more.

You alone know this secret and if you tell it with your body, the other bodies will not believe you.

Your power will set free all the martyrs imprisoned under the churches. Bodies that have no peace yet, bound by men of antiquity in labyrinthine catacombs.

With eyes and fingers you will speak to splendid images of love, and silvered smiles will dress you in rustles.

But how many explanations you require!

Observe, observe the painting from different distances. Distinguish, divide, devour the monstrous images, dwell in their place ...

Like these candelabra in the desert, anchored without flame to boundless clouds.[7]

Who are you? Stone chessboard ... who is playing with you?

Deeds done – not to be understood now – lead to solitude and astonishment.

I shall kill you and then I shall corrupt you. Tomorrow infinite new cities will arise from the opposites.

Pain indifferently and stoically borne due to the shameful flight of the troops. General, I am staying.

---

7 With reference to Dovilio Brero's painting "The Great Work."

Thirty-three is the number of the hypogeum. I shall leap now to new stars or the descent will be steep.

The birch will again be used, as it once was used by the Celts to flog the boys. Upon the branches of the white wood swing twelve Rusalki still holding the memory of their own violent deaths.[8]

Beware travelers! You will find them in the darkest corners, or behind bright, blinding leaves, ready to make you die laughing. But perhaps, this tree will save you again.

Frail creatures! A mattress of birch will give life to the bones and every evil will be driven far from the fire against the dark spirits.

Traitors are those who in time reconsider – out of personal interest – what today is crystal clear.

Judas, in words decried by the church fathers, held back gestures that more clearly speak his mind: 4, 2, 5, 6. [9]

But whoever is aware of the error, do they have sufficient modesty to obey and grow? Or do they stay confined, puffed up with presumption and insanity, farther and farther away from the sacred rites? Forever?

Is a body without thought in Maya, just experiencing the illusion of being alive because of spasms – the electrical reactions and jerks of a dead frog?

---

[8] In Slavic mythology, Rusalki are female water nymphs, demons or mermaids who like to lure humans to a drowning death.

[9] 4, 2, 5, 6 are numbers representing an answer received from *The Book of Synchronicity*, a divinatory tool created by Falco and referenced herein to offer the reader additional clues for *The Game of Life*. The book is available at Amazon and as an iPad app.

What is LIFE?

Is it freedom to choose? What is right and what is wrong? Is it perhaps a relationship of forces?

Daphne refused the love of Apollo and was transformed into a laurel.[10] It is written in the *Vedas* that Urvashi, a beautiful young nymph, would not surrender to the love of the sun, the High Pururavas, and she too became a sweet-smelling laurel ... which in order to exist needs the sun.[11]

Why could they not seize the instant, the gesture in the moment, gifted by the synchronic power, and explode into higher universes? Did an upbringing that imprisons and takes away strength hold back their Being?

The hunter with a single arrow knows that if he hesitates when his prey flies past and miss-shoots, he will no longer be able to hit anything. He will die. He will no longer have any strength, any prey, any life.

Without that, the value of Being is limited.

Zela, you tell me now: How much of you and of me would you give, Divine One, to enter into Time? Does not this disorder attract you, the boiling of souls bubbling up, their struggles to rise toward us? And one day, surpass us?

Instinctive rituals are to be respected, even in everyday actions. If I were to place a sacred crystal on the altar in a certain manner, I should surely mark this day in white; but if I don't respect the synchronic message, bad will come to me as a result, and a black stone will mark out this date.

---

[10] Greek mythology.
[11] Hindu mythology.

And then, the body remembers everything: If a year ago one's flesh was wounded, today, although healthy, it remembers and it hurts. And the liver, the stomach, in the eternal conversation on nourishment, also remember the dates of important events.

If you read in a book, "All books are untrue," and believe firmly in those words, you will, in time, be tied to causality.

And if you do not believe in those words, but believe in what you read, then you will again, in time, be tied to causality.

The Major Arcana and all the seventy-eight signs speak the Truth. Not the method, but the moment teaches and speaks. Only the symbol is needed and now it shall be: 1, 3, 3, 3 – it is you.

Fight like a kitten among the dogs, without hope yet with absolute confidence. Get scratched, become, transform yourself into what does not yet exist ... and never has.

Why do you cry? Come into my arms, little creature. I'll stroke your hair, the back of your neck, I'll give you a big hug and, maybe, I'll tickle you.

Tears of pain, of helplessness, of dejection. (In secret you'll hug my photo, or these friendly pages.)

Do the others not see your sweetness? Do they keep you at a distance? Your warm tears, do they count for nothing?

Lost, tender creature, if you stamp your feet three times you'll see things change! The sea of your pain will start to calm.

These are not cold words, little ageless being! Have you seen how your soul, forever childlike, has been imprisoned in this wrinkled, withered, worn out body? Have you seen how the years left you small while your body grew, filled out, procreated? Old child! Your whims are always the same, masked by experience and appearances.

Show how grown up you are. Don't cry, don't despair. The cup is half-full, not half-empty. Clothe yourself with yellow, with life and smiles. Without tears, your soul is lighter. The last tremors are passing, have a final sniffle.

My rings, you know, have two settings: that of trust and that of defense.

The word and the information: Consciousness and Knowledge.

A ritual, like the air, unites all the creatures of the world, ring-bound to one another.

I shall answer you, Alfo: I see this pain, down there, and its essence escapes me. How will they ever be able to compete with us, these animated things? They'll get naught of me for a particle of Time!

Mintha, daughter of Cocytus, loved and was loved by Hades. Jealous Persephone turned her into mint.[12]

Times and resurrections. Temples rebuilt.

In the previous cycle, this herb was sacred to Isis and Thoth. In the Temple of Horus at Edfu, the priests prepared the sacred Kyphi, distilling with secret formulas this miraculous unguent, which drives away death and defeats disease.

---

[12] Greek mythology.

In Asia, its perfume is an aphrodisiac and in Turkey the herb prolongs life. It is born of the underworld to give more life ...

Why are important things born of the transgressions of superhuman beings? Why does Zeus find an opportunity in incest, between Oxylus and his sister, to transform the nymph into a walnut tree?[13]

What is the metamorphosis that takes place among human beings, trees, and Gods that turns humans into Gods and renders Gods more human?

The olive is sacred to Athena and only its wood may be burned on her altars.

An olive seed is on the tomb of Adam, placed by the Archangel that guards the doors of Paradise.[14]

Olive is the wood of the cross of Christ.

The dove bore a twig in its beak to Noah ...

Trees and men, in a millennial merry-go-round, together play chess with the Gods.

I see great tears go by on the road. Bright as steel, tears of Mercury as large as men slide along the pavements. What do you have inside of you, creature?

Your secret wealth remains hidden from the sun, wrapped in clouds of modesty and poor self-esteem.

Birds cry on the roofs and in the squares of crumbling cities. In response, men and children cry to the heavens.

---

[13] Greek mythology: Oxylus and his sister Hamadryas gave birth to eight tree nymphs.

[14] Christian mythology.

I distractedly threw the days of my life into the Game. Out of boredom, I didn't take part in the dawns and sunsets. I used to sigh, leaning on my elbow, playing around with dates, days, seasons.

My chain let me go from home to the bar, to work. More and more often I would stop thinking. Every noise was an excuse for not doing.

Then pain shook my uselessness. I threw away talents and picked up rubbish. I thought I was someone who had life all figured out: 3, 6, 6, 6.

Now already too many memories are surfacing for my liking. Does it mean I am old?

It still has a funny effect on me to remember and find myself saying, "twenty years ago." Either my memory has gotten longer, or a lot of years truly have gone by.

Yet another life has rounded the promontory and lazily sails out into the open sea. So it is, for many.

Yellowed school notebooks, loves, promises, sudden wisps of unfortunate desires.

I shall never live in the memory of you; it could be regret. Jealousy perhaps, but only of the idea. How can one be jealous of what is dead?

From one life the soul bounds to another and the planet whirls, there, around the sun.

I return, I am reborn, in secret I grow inside a new body.

I manifest the "me" for the work that awaits me.

I meet with you again, my lover most sweet. In Imperial Rome, in the Yucatan, in the north and the south of the world …

Where there are deserts, there used to be forests and endless fields and golden and red and white cities.

Where there is desolation, there were shouts of joy and songs and young lives. Moments from an eternity.

I shall grow old among my animals, seven years at a time. They know. They recognized me immediately when they came to stay with me again.

And still you, old dog. Hesitating, you wait for me by the window in the morning, when I open the eyes of the house. The other one whines by the door. It's no use remaining silent and holding my breath – she knows.

And you, water flowers, lovely as the first day: Rejoice in me as I am gladdened by you.

I talk to you and your eyes roll around and go dull. You hear only your ghosts.

Do you still talk to the dead? Endless ritual conversations. You believe, old man, that you are with mommy and daddy. They live again in some dusty corner, there in the back of your brain.

You smile and gesticulate and talk in tongues that are no more.

It is pointless, making yourself so busy if you know nothing of the human world.

You know all about law, about medicine and literature, the atoms have no more secrets. Yet you don't know what it is that you feel for her.

The plant in the pot twists toward the sun. You imperceptibly turn toward the idea of love.

Your first wrinkles, now, won't iron themselves out. Time filters your body as the stars remain in their place.

Youth is a silly idea, inflated with useless regrets. How old are you? What have you still left in the tank? How many years per hour can you do? And with one liter?

Of what use are these confused words with no apparent link between them?
Who on earth are YOU

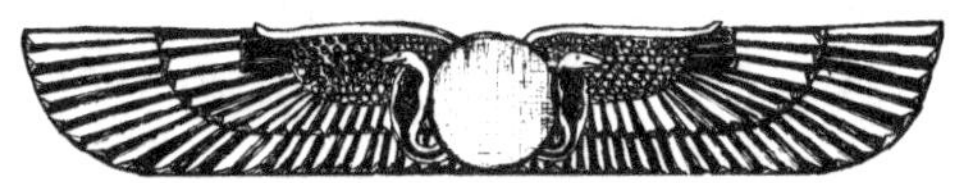

PART TWO: LESSONS
Inspirations from a Prophet

One day, an Initiate to the mysteries wanted to judge and choose whether or not to carry on along the sacred path. But for this very reason, he was excluded from it.

Can a man decide whether he wants to stop the sun?

My carpets are the four elements of the world. At times they are joined, at times not.

The trophy memories from so many lives are masks. Do not flee but sail barefoot through the present and through the adventure of the body. So many images, impressions and sensations.

Zela, listen: What if their moment were eternal, every instant lived to the full as it is here, on the carpets of the world?

If the teaching touched them, across the bridge sent between the absolute and the finite.

If they overcame the distances between the body and the subtle light animating them, even though suffering wounds of pure pain.

So then: Could they not manage to compete with us? Would it not appear like harmony, that struggling of theirs?

So set yourself free from all fears. Make a clear flag of your repressed smiles. Caress and love sweetly like a triumphant Krishna.

Give joy and look into the eyes, read the eyes. Wave your hands around when you talk and put the whole of your being into it.

Speak out, without fear of ridicule, what you're feeling and living inside. Kiss softly without caring what the slaves will say about you.

From a dry drop of blood on the Shroud, it is possible to clone the Christ and make the man Jesus live again.

From a tooth of Buddha, the Buddha will take shape again, a man among men, without the soul of an Initiate but full of natural gifts. And so for Muhammad.

You're astonished at growing old, this hair that was thicker yesterday. And your hands are strange and different. Yet you always have had them; you should be used to them.

Don't distance yourself from everyone, but stay with yourself. And above all, don't cry. It's no good anymore.

Search in the dark with hands anxious to touch. Look carefully at everything, every side, every color, and then open your eyes.

Don't threaten any more those you have offended. Your gestures are sufficient, indeed excessive. The rages of others are born from your superficiality and their compressed problems. Comprehend.

Old man
with unsteady step
you hesitate
and hold out your hands
you start again
and hesitate once more.

The whole world taps out rhythms, reassuring as a sucked thumb. Your heart marks time and acts as the musical backdrop, like in a movie, to the whole of your life.

Every action has its own rhythm, now dramatic, now calm, now poetic. You are your music: puffing and counterpoint of voices, background drum, foot-beats, hands, voice.

Lungs, intestinal alchemies and jaws, teeth, touching and bones. These are our sounds and instruments for the daily dance.

Stifling like the summer heat, between the rows of vines: So is the breath of old age.

You would shift your old bones with the effort of a laborer moving a wheelbarrow of sand, uphill. And yet yesterday, you jumped to your feet, you ran like what you were – a child. You slipped through half-shut doors fast as a tiger cat!

Now you pause with every step. And your voice has worn out. It huffs like an over-played record.

Mistrusting, from the real or imagined blows of life, you drag yourself along, alone like a tuft of hair on your head, abandoned by so many companions.

If you are wise, you can laugh at yourself.

When you have exhausted your curiosity, my respectful and admired disciple, you will cast me aside like an old newspaper you've done with reading.

Then it will be presumption guiding your path.

In Truth, you will have learned many curious notions but not the essence of my words, or philosophy ... whatever you want to call it.

If you are tied to things, if you are not WHOLE, if you don't become a nomad, with all your things where you are, always in you, if the best day of your life is not now, you will have lost time, missed the train, lost yourself (you will hardly get around by bike).

You will judge and you will not be judged. Oh how much more time I've got than you!

You will never enter my paintings, neither as object, nor as beast. You will have the empty spirit of the frame!

Alfo, now, in the eternal now that is our field, I shall cast, synchronically, a handful of seeds, scattered along the furrow of Time. They will germinate into nations and among the humans, civilizations. The divine seeds will be Prophets, Envoys, sons of Gods and Gods themselves. They will gather handfuls of pain, they will sieve grains of wisdom from this cup, this grail, which I shall break and cast among the seeds, upon the world.

So be it. I am the Beginning, on High, Mother Generatrix of all things, thought of thought, sword and shield, tree, chaos ... chance.

A Divine Spark has flown through the world, gliding down like a seagull between wind and sea.

They are filled with it, those few whose sight, right then, was set upon the high heavens.

Otherwise, they are all blind. So many, many, many, many words – not primordial and so not pure and divine – gravitate like fog and hide the sun.

From the Divine Eye has blazed, did blaze, is blazing an unbroken branching river, its banks lined with trees of good and evil, laden with apples of wisdom.

They are sterile fruits for the human form, except for one every two thousand years.

Rivers of symbols run up and down the sky. Colored handkerchiefs, similar to flags, flutter as a reference to the important things of the world.

Cascades of words submerge seas of multitudes of men.

Tempting hells change the cards on the table of humanity drained of its blood.

Colored pencils trace stories lived in particles of time and seasons by women in love. Thoughts explode. Words are loaded with compromises.

Little households become nations and great states ... miserable hovels. A glance from the Gods wipes out the most defended planets and unassailable planetary fortresses.

The mind of the seeded one remains free and inviolate. He senses the ages whirl about his bodies, young and old, season upon season. His smiles and humorous glances escape most people, even those who surround him with veneration.

Such is not real understanding, even though, usually, it is the planets closest to the sun that are the warmest and the most illuminated.

Understanding a word that touches the boundaries of one's own comfort is as difficult as ever, and if it brushes against the fetters of one's own upbringing and moral conditioning, it is worse still.

Zela, you have emitted what the I-We thought had deliberated: It is right. We shall contemplate from this window of time the eras of when and where. Upon your seeds, follows my rain.

The Game wanted by who is above us has begun. The bridge sent, therefore, will spring from your seed and from my water. They might annihilate themselves or surpass us, just as it has been thought. Will it be harmony, the alchemical mixing of so many ingredients?

Why, Zela, have you decided in favor of what previously you opposed?

I have slipped between the widest of spirals and incommensurable spaces.

The I-Consciousness has condensed into letters and words, the words into texts. The opportunities of the world have reared different, minuscule worlds, each one of them contemplating, containing, and contained by spinning quasi-reals and indefinable colors.

What do these words mean? In which world, or river, or reply is the key kept?

How many parables does it take to explain the inexplicable: color to the blind, music to the deaf, speed to snails, flight to earthworms, open air to the fish of the abyss?

The dreamer remembers mountains of clouds.

Do not cross my path, solitary bird; do not cross my path. The journey to the clouds is as long as your existence. When you get there, they are made of nothing, illusion, Maya ...

Being is the only Truth.

Taking part is illusion yet fundamental for this existence. The rail track continues its run forever.

Papers old with news still fly and trickle down between the tracks, just like fistfuls of seagulls flung between the roads of the sky.

A New Force

Now then, the ant who discovered fire took the news of her great discovery to the queen and her minions. Of course no one believed her. But all the insects, invited and lured by this enthusiast, went to the place of the miracle.

Alas, nothing shone anymore, nothing caught fire anymore in front of the magic drop. The little ant was the target of jokes and derision on the part of her companions and punished by the queen.

The following day, a beautiful sunny day, the ant went to meditate in front of the dewdrop, which hung like shiny, ripe fruit from a long blade of grass. And still around, several insects watched her from a distance, giggling, making fun of her. In Truth, they did not know why they watched – some were curious, others were drawn by the mystery.

She tried, tried again to put tiny little pieces of leaf, as votive offerings, in front of the drop ... nothing happened.

She prayed; she waited. Time passed and the sun rose higher and higher in the sky. Several curious companions had tired of waiting and had gone away. Others had come and stood around, fascinated by her words of prayer. Some even carried twigs and bits of dried leaves to help her.

She too was tired by now.

Then the sun reached the exact position, the rays were concentrated, and a pale, fine stream of smoke burst lazily from the little votive heap. Synchronically, the flame lighted with a light gust of wind!

Those who laughed were dumbfounded. Those who contributed with toil to the strange work of the little ant redoubled their efforts.

This time, others had witnessed the miracle and everyone swarmed around to tell that it was true, as it was true – the sun had appeared on the earth.

But when the queen arrived with the rest of the anthill, nothing more happened. Not knowing how to control their new power, they had let the fire go out. There remained only a little pile of ashes, the symbol and *vibhuti* of the ants who had been converted to the idea of the New Force.

Another day went by, dark clouds raced across the sky, hiding the sun. All the ants waited for the magic time when the sacred fire would miraculously burst into flame.

But the sky was getting darker and darker. At the destined time, nothing happened.

Consequently, many of the ants who had embraced the New Force recanted their faith. They instigated others and became the leaders of those who were attacking the few remaining faithful.

The bearer of the idea of fire tried to explain why it was not the moment of the miracle: that the sun was the

source of everything. But she was merely laughed at and persecuted.

In the following days, the little heroine discovered that if she climbed onto a blade of grass and used threads of cobweb, it was possible to change the position of the drop in relation to the sun.

She also learned, with the help of her companions, to carry little drops of water in folded leaves to make bigger drops where needed. She discovered sunnier spots and how to place well dried twigs at the meeting point of the concentrated rays. She learned how to dry the twigs in the wind, how to press them down well, and how to waft the air with little pieces of leaves so as to make the fire catch light better.

All this knowledge, these rites, seemingly meaningless dances, were kept secret and cultivated in secret.

With the art of fire, the faithful discovered over time that when the fire is great, some small stones fuse and make metals. They discovered that some crystals serve the same function as the drops of water. And that wood hardens in the flames to become a powerful weapon to defend themselves against their enemies. That the ash is an excellent fertilizer for cultivating underground mushrooms and for preserving winter foods longer, keeping sickness at bay, molds, and a thousand other things.

They learned to trace secret signs, to recall to mind the techniques and knowledge.

They invented writing, by engraving different little signs on tough leaves with their jaws. With the wax of the bees, they preserved the sacred books containing the new knowledge. And they taught the faithful to read and write.

The ants learned to attract night butterflies with the fire and to tame them, and they also taught them to carry the faithful to faraway places or high up in the trees, effortlessly.

The religion-knowledge born of the Victorious Sun gave them the powers of the New Force, and with it an ever higher spiritual awareness.

First secretly, then openly, they preached that it was possible to bring the sun onto the earth. Believing they were doing right, they gave a small part of their science to the anthill, to see if the whole community was ready for the revelations of the secrets of the New Force.

Straightaway, the ant soldiers discovered unthinkable, exalting possibilities for the use of fire. They saw that they could set upon the conquest of other anthills with the threat of destruction. And so they did. Crazy generals attacked their presumed enemies with fire and easily overwhelmed all defense.

But the fire spread out of their control and set the whole wood alight, threatening their own anthill at close quarters. Only the faithful followers of the New Force managed to escape, taking the pure of heart with them. Seeing ahead, they realized that power should not be used unless the Consciousness and Knowledge of those who employ it has risen above bestiality.

Are the wars among the ants the cause of the mysterious fires in the woods?

So the ant followers of the New Force formed secret societies in many anthills, to prepare for the coming of the Great Awakening of the whole species.

In their monastery, the arts assumed great importance.

They learned to dig down into the hard rock, to light up the darkest of places with little mirrors of quartz. They frescoed the walls of the underground villages with exquisite art. They became poets, artists of the most refined culture. Every new work and every new discovery was to the greater glory of their faith.

They were closely united with the source of things: the Unvanquished Sun, bearer of life, joy, evolution. But what a sacrifice and commitment, to create the liberation of their world!

Alfo, my material dream will prove in the Divine Game how much these creatures can create from small drops of Knowledge.

We, ourselves Gods, are subject to greater Gods and dreams, in eternal harmonies.

You, yourself, now seem to hesitate about the greatness of our accomplishment. Let us observe, then.

I believe that mothers are much more dangerous for their children than germs.

The antibiotic a mother gives her son to cure the fever that frightens her, cures her fear but not his health. Her son pays for her fear with his life or with parts of his life.

Is this not true?

Your eyes, deadened of Knowledge, freeze the things that smile. Your anxieties cause a vibration of fear which secretly frightens the men and women of the world, yet you believe they cannot detect it.

Thus, the fear of failure places spiritual barriers upon the maturity of whoever fears.

My caresses are the synchronic fruit of the night wind. For your sake, I desire joy without ties.

What is lived with purity is pure. The leaves of the forest welcome the drops, heavenly kisses, burning diamonds outside of time.

The hearth fire dances for us, in the night, fantastic melodies, languid and desperate.

Fireplace

Upon the burning stage
each piece of wood
gives the best of itself.

There are no two flames the same. Nor memories the same. I can go back to the past, remember thousands of faces, lives, eras, situations.

As an exile in Rome, at the home of a woman who took me in. During the rebellions of a forgotten African empire – the grassy plains of the Sahara and its red and white cities and golden rivers. Further back, when the Italian glaciers quivered with life and came creaking down to slip into the Piedmont seas.

The ages, the wars, the cities destroyed and built a hundred times over. The kings, lords of the world, now without name.

The sands of time that erode the monuments through the millennia mark not my soul. I have negotiated with young Gods, tasted the sweet apple of Adam, forged the fiery sword of the avenging angel.

I have advised and served countless lords, kings, emperors of the world. Suggested inventions, stimulated discoveries, preached religions. I have consulted sibyls and I have been consulted.

I have seen thousand year old trees grow and become old. I have dug out mountains, erected temples, killed and fought endless times.

I carry the message distilled from all the ages.

My faith prefers these commandments:

Curiosity: Human beings are curious and explorers. They can seek and explore.

Knowledge: Human beings can then turn curiosity into Knowledge. By doing so, they increase their power and ability to act. Thus, they have more free will. Hence, greater evolution.

Consciousness: At the end of Knowledge matures the Consciousness of Being, absolute Truth, self-education. Finally, mature Consciousness educates the human being in the adult and responsible use of Knowledge.

On the subtle planes, Consciousness leads to memory, to the soul, to God. Through this path, awareness leads to joy, to the divine humor which is born of comprehension.

It is not an easy road but a clear one.

Respect for those who have little Consciousness makes us go through pain, but it is worth it, for the whole of Humankind.

That's it. That will do for today.

I have just about laid the foundations of a new religion.

PART THREE: KNOWLEDGE
The Path to Enlightenment

We do not need the miracle of a drop of Knowledge to create a New Force. Each drop is contained within every one of us.

Another season is going by, rich with ancient news: Winter makes seeds mature, spring will bring life and a joyous, irrepressible desire to smile.

How we are slaves of our sad habits!

He who is alone creates his personal rituals to face the known-unknown of every day. It is a good thing, because synchronically, a few conscious gestures make the day and the subtle forces of chance favorable.

The flower in the earthenware pot is watching me, curious and thoughtful. I respond to its thoughts, and its aura shines with amazement. It pulls back, has another go, and again I respond to it. Cheers to you, bearer of colors!

In the human being, nature has brought together herbivore and carnivore, hunter and hunted. It is certainly an interesting experiment.

A flash of genius for this planet created the form that is ours in this existence: primates and carnivores in one. Bridges between the animal realms, as well as bridges between the material and subtle ones, beyond the body.

I really long for friends – true human friends – to whom I may give all of me without asking. Companions, brothers and sisters, whom I shower with affection, with sweet and secret favors. Respectful people whom I respect and value for what they humanly are.

Playing together, telling one another things without danger, mistaken thoughts, or betrayals. Companions of happy times and difficult times. Sitting down together while the table is set and then united in joy, hospitality, and fondness. Sharing more serious and personal topics, aware that my home is their home.

Friends whose greatest gift is their heart, a joke, a witty line. As human as this planet is human. It is the need for play that is most lacking, outside social conventions suited to strangers.

I give without asking, as long as I have. My finest day is always today. The smile of a friend is the summer in between two harsh winters. It is a beautiful song after the din of the city traffic.

But what is the value of friendship?

A friend does not declare his own merits. A friend is there when you need him or her. He knows how to stay silent, when to speak, whether to listen, and how to reveal himself.

I know of relationships between friends carried on from one lifetime to another and of marriage left unresumed beyond a single existence ...

Punch the pessimist on the nose, so that his ideas are confirmed. And hug every optimist, so that they can be surer still of what they feel.

Launch a crusade in favor of those who hope, feel, believe, and you will see euphoria, celebration. Launch another against those who despair, and you will see black, mourning, and ruin.

Render unto Caesar that which is Caesar's.

I have drawn magical designs on parchment paper that I made myself. Shapes and figures and colors have sprung forth, calls to cosmic energies.

The magical design attracts curious Gods. Words and gestures, as ancient as I, have found a place in the universe.

I have clasped hands with my selves through the mirror, while Adams and Eves continue being tempted by legions of serpents, on plantations of apple trees.

The suns have repeatedly risen at each dawn on the horizons, sometimes on the right and sometimes on the left. They have become tiny and have filled the whole sky with fire.

My face and body are changing with the years; I can see it before the mirror. Inside I am still the same boy.

I mature alongside the experiences of the world, and swim between events and seasons.

Time and again, I keep my millennial secret, as I wander through the 333 rooms of the enchanted and accursed castle.

I sing the vowels and the colors. I cast thoughts, sowing fresh minds.

Why so many words without a logical sequence?
It is the thought of every day, of every minute, that plays with circumstances ...
Now I am present, right now.

Don't worry, frail love, I feel the good that is in you. It is not useless, you are not in an alley with no exits.
You need not hold back your tears and emotions now. Sob for yourself, for what is past: epochs, events, faces lost in time, flashes of memory, regrets for things never done and words not spoken when the moment was right ...
Let the sobs free you from the misunderstandings. From the days when you were restrained and silent and let others insult you. From rages that you unjustly endured. From words you never wish to hear again ...
Listen, frail creature, your strength has brought you here. Now pass over the bridge and get on the train – the only train in the station – and come to me!
Don't flee.
Meet. Win. Now!

Without the help of my children, my heart will beat only so long as my hair is dark.
I should study for them, not work for them.
I should speak, relate, and teach what I know, with whatever time is left to me, whatever time they will concede me ...

Epitaph

*Here smiles a man
who has searched for imagination and for freedom.
Believing he had found it all,
he tried to teach it to others.*

*For some he is an Envoy,
and they will pray and heal upon this tomb.
Time will be the judge and prove,
right beyond question,
those who have understood his message.*

The planarians that feed on the bodies of their companions acquire their memories.

Thus, whosoever wishes can bring to memory the experiences of thousands of lives, without directly participating in them, by feeding on the spirits of the dead.

How many subtle bodies (and not so subtle) are imprisoned within rotting corpses? What would you give, dead ones, that I should help you to escape matter?

Fire, sweet master of my senses, you twist around and perform upon a stage of embers. You trace fantastic figures of sumptuous fables.

With you, I am always the old beast that has been watching you in fascination for a million years. You have been the faithful companion of men on joyous and dangerous hunts. You have been support and warmth and safety.

You have been fear and the destruction of my cities.

Fire, you have been the means of transforming matter into divine essence. You have been the path by which we approached the Gods. You have been the why, the how, and the wherefore.

You are a constant, in all my existences.

You alone, fire, know how to keep so well my thoughts and the secrets of the world.

With your dances, for thousands of years, you have communicated dreams to Humankind. You have told us what to dream, you have told us what to feel, you have told us what to invent.

Few are aware of the fact that you are a real, living creature, living on a faster plane than our human one. Few are able to recognize in you a thinking and living being.

I have known your rage and your bite.

I have been consumed on the pyre.

I have seen your fury, in the woods and between the walls of the cities.

We have become friends, and like friends we tell one another everything, keeping each other's secrets.

Smoke, your brother, is of a different nature. As much as you are warm and bright, he is obscure and dense. As much as you are fast and lively, he is slow and suffocating.

The nets which weave space have caught suns and planets ...

One day a worm, writhing around as much as it could amid a thousand sufferings, managed to turn over and see the heavens for the first time. It remained fascinated.

"Oh, how much I would like to browse among those blue meadows, in that blue grass," it said. "Instead, I'm down here in the mud and amidst a thousand dangers, with birds spying on me! Why can't I be one of them? A hunter, rather than a prey?"

Then the worm began to meditate. It studied for a long time, suffered, then carried on crawling, searching for its path.

One day a voice said to the worm, "You are ready," and wove a cocoon around its mortal body. The worm prayed again for a long, long time, until at last, it came forth from the silky coffin and changed into a butterfly.

The splendid, luminous creature flew toward the heavens, toward the sun.

"Look," it said, "Now I have renewed myself. I have become, at last, what I desired and the heavens are my pasture, my meadow."

A bird arrived, swiftly, seized the worm and ate it.

Its body became food, whereas its soul, part of the bird.

Those who prepare their existence through obedience, through the awareness of remaining upright and consistent with what they have sworn, are ready for the kingdom of the heavens – and for every transformation that follows – such that they may reach the infinite peak of the pyramid.

Even for the last to arrive there is great hope, and not just for those who for a long time have been opening the road to others. Whoever has begun the path will have sound help from those who, arriving as fresh forces, have more energy to carry on and attain new levels, new powers, new forms ... KNOWLEDGE.

It also is written that he who enters the vineyard at the eleventh hour will have a whole day's pay. Thus, those who arrive last on the train, if they have good will, can be among the first in the kingdom that will be created on earth and in the heavens. Prophetic words!

Time will reveal the true and distinguish it from the false.

A Story

A long time ago, Humankind used to dominate space. Their proud form had power on many worlds.

However, what happened then is happening once again: The technology of humans surpassed and was not suited to their insufficient and meager spiritual knowledge. And yet, mankind could still travel in space if they navigated on the Synchronic Lines which join suns and planets, galaxies and other systems. In this way, they could transfer their essence into other bodies on other worlds.

This is the real journey within the universe.

The idea of spaceships sailing through nothingness to carry goods is a barbaric thought that makes any evolved alien smile. It is not goods, it is not matter that is important in space. It is information. It is ideas.

Only commerce in Knowledge counts, since matter is the same in every part of the universe. Through Knowledge, anything can be built in any part of the infinite!

Zela, I see the times and the thoughts set in material motion by what was willed. Let us contemplate the eras and the fruits of the race mind of Humankind.

How curious: Every now and then I appear to get a fleeting feeling of deja vu, of deja lived. Consciousness of unconsciousness, flashes of thoughts fished up from the fantasies and efforts of these creatures come in waves toward us. And at times, among these illusions, there blossoms a fruit filled with the juice of power.

Yes, it's true, I hesitate. I also am amazed at times by how much Knowledge has moved through us.

The step has been taken. The Game of Life is marshalling its ranks of enlightenable ones ...

PART FOUR: THE GAME
Rules and Stories

The Game of Life exalts and destroys, annihilates and rebuilds. It makes, disappears, and creates. Every individual can be reborn through it. Every being can rise from its own ashes.

There are no limits or brakes on human will. And when necessary, different replies are given to the same question.

Desire is born from the lack of love, from the selfishness of those who have their eyes closed. Desire becomes the need for power, and power makes a slave of those who use it, as much as those who are subjugated by it.

A harp among the stars can produce wonderful symphonies.

Every star is the mirror of a human being, a musical note. Every note has its right tempos, pauses and appropriate beats ...

According to the early Christians, Christ initiated his mission during the Jewish Jubilee, and that is true. What better moment than that to redistribute the land, to activate the five hundred year revolution, to free the slaves, to spread new ideas?

Also, Dante began his infernal journey with the Roman Jubilee in 1300 C.E.

Today, when the Jubilees have disappeared under the sign of the shell on the shoulder. Today, when eight is the number of infinity, of the awakening of Horus, of the beginning of the Age of Aquarius. Today, in this moment, I celebrate the awakening of the New Human Being.

The initiation of the travelers of the spirit speeds up and gets more intense. The sacred auspices are positive and the Black Forces gather resources to attack us.

Will the army flee this time or will it be able to stand up to and defeat the Enemy of Humankind? Will humans toast to their own true liberation with the cup of gold, keeping watch with joy, working with faith, learning something every day?

What have you learned today, dear Reader?.

I will stroke dark, blond, and white heads, thick or thin of hair. I will have smiles and substantial help for all the children of all the fathers and all the mothers of the world.

I will take away the "o" and the "s" of *chaos* and turn it into *chance.*[15]

I will call on the Gods to help me watch over myself, to quash the doubts coming from the Enemy, and to examine

---

[15] The Italian word *caos* (chaos) is an anagram of *caso* (chance).

in depth those coming from myself. I will not be afraid of myself. I will love myself a little ...

I will take care of my appearance to offer a harmonious and clean image to the sensitivity that I respect in others.

I will provide food and friendship. My home will be for everyone and I will be at home at everyone's home.

I will give wrong answers to repeated questions. I will trick, I will test and stimulate minds to force them to form.

I will call for arts, music, design. I will want statues and books from my friends.

I will expect my companions to be harmonious, happy, and hard working. Stimulating, spirited replies, clever solutions, intelligent jokes will always be welcome. Rest for the body, yes, and varied and tasty food, theater, and songs – everything to form new cultures.

Always, we must be ready to start everything again from scratch!

I have suffered the cold for you; the frost has dug into my bones. I have suffered the heat for you; it has calcified my bones.

From the stars, I have faithfully reproduced the selfic spirals that link the immense to the minute.

The correspondence of the stellar forces is at your service through the little object you wear on yourself.[16]

I know how to build life ...

---

[16] With reference to the personal synchronic selfic device that Damanhurians use. Selfica is an ancient discipline that makes it possible to convey and direct intelligent energies that have a beneficial effect on the person and the environment.

The universe is my home. The darkness and the cold of space are my habitual breath, my cradle, the only place where I feel eternally safe, outside of time.

I float in the nothingness that fills the void between the worlds.

Far away from me, suns and galaxies burn and consume themselves. Eternal, my principle matures and evolves ...

There are no mists of time able to hold me back. There is no matter able to chain me. There are no roads other than that of my will.

I am everyone and no one.

Joy pervades the universe and dances among galaxies drunk with celestial music ...

I navigate between your questions, oh, Lanoo, like an expert chess player, with a pupil.[17] There are no reefs to my teaching, there are no limits to your understanding.

I teach FREEDOM. And freedom is attained through renouncing one's desire for the things of the world.

You cannot judge, Lanoo, but you can be judged.

Every choice happens through considerations that are not yours. Time is the only valid judge and what seems wrong to you now, tomorrow may turn out to be your salvation.

Christianity arose three centuries after the death of the Christ, set in motion by the nails of the cross.

Who can judge in time, but the one who sent the Initiate Man-Christ? Who could foresee the consequences, but the Lords who determined with their power and will

---

[17] Lanoo is a level of initiation at Damanhur's School of Meditation.

that Jesus was a good choice for this world? And yet the good of the planet is still far off, considering the events of today ...

Those who are immersed in time cannot consider the reality of the facts with a sharp, clear mind, just as a person who is drowning cannot judge the sea.

You, who are indeed escaping from your problems, who consider your children as your property, remember: They do not belong to you. You have given them a body but the soul comes from much, much, further away.

And if they are, according to you, rebelling, maybe you are mistaken. Rather, they are looking for their own experience.

You want their assurance that the road you took and walked in the wrong way will not be changed. How can you be sure that for them, indeed, the opposite cannot happen? Different times! Different conditions!

And your children: What if they have the courage of their actions? If they manage to make spiritual choices, you are truly a fortunate parent. From your flesh something beautiful was born which will carry your name throughout time like no other family, not even the noblest or oldest.

Every light in the night can be friendly or hostile, according to your state of mind.

Trees can clutch at you and pursue you, or be your only protection.

Voices and sounds in the night can be bearers of mysteries, danger and of unspeakable horrors, or give you a sweet and tender sense of the warm security and friendliness of the world.

Who are you then, human being, looking for your essence? What divine voice has touched your mind, your sensitive and yet unknown antennae?

Why do you turn and turn again with the same old reassuring questions, asked more out of superstition than out of a will to know?

You must not search at all costs for satisfying certainties, but rather for crystal clear Truths.

If Truth is a crystal and every consideration a facet, the more facets you discover, the more Knowledge you have … and the more Truth you possess.

Try to touch yourself, to feel your flesh. Now, you may feel yourself, but do you know yourself?

What "God" has spoken to your soul? Which entity has engraved questions on your spirit such that you uselessly look for his tiring answers?

Why do you live in this manner?

In human terms, which is worth more to you: a conversation carried on with your tongue clacking on and on against the roof of your mouth and teeth, or your tongue clinched around another tongue in a deep, sweet, passionate and tender kiss?

And this thick snow, will it allow your soul to peacefully bud in the field where it was sown?

Oh, Gods, listen to my voice! I lift up my arms and my head, and I am wearing the robe of my grade.

I have lit a fire of white wood and a fire of black wood, so that you can hear my voice.

I, yes, a simple person, can speak with you! I can negotiate with you!

Gods who have tricked Humankind, who wanted to punish my mother Eve when she uncovered your lies!

When, with amazement, you discovered that these creatures – to whom you gave life and from whom you receive life – could become immortal! When you chased them away, filled with terror, because the apple of wisdom had already been picked ...

Gods, listen to me! Negotiate with me, and my trusty and powerful Divine allies! Even the Gods of the sea are with me!

Renew the pact with Humankind, without any humiliating clauses. And let this pact be respected until the end of time.

Through the Synchronic Lines whose portal I know and control – hear me! My voice vibrates in the universe through the lines and the antennae of the magical network that coil and twine around every inhabited world.

This is the prophesied moment!

I have broken in two the arrow that transforms events, that strikes and kills or does not strike at all, depending on where it is shot.

Here the road of the probables comes to a fork and originates new branches, up and along time.

And so I can watch events and follow the declarations of faith. I can listen to congregations of roosters, crowing their cries of betrayal, and of dogs biting the hand that feeds them.

But I also can see the unshakeable certainty and trust of a handful of conquerors, searchers for the grail, hunters

of initiation, travelers for Enlightenment who are living the eternal present of the moment ...

The false prophet will tell of the end of humanity and make thousands of predictions. He will tell you that the vital choice incarnated in the present body is not an active participant in the Game, that the breathing lung and the beating heart are not life, but survival.

Such superficiality kills Consciousness, as does stupidity. It is the winter of existence, this age. The slow, freezing breath of distraction is in minds and hearts.

Those who show the way are opposed by murderous disbelief. Eyes are shut and heads hidden in the sand like a child who, in order to disappear, closes his eyes and believes he is invisible because *he* cannot see.

Mantra of Time

E intanto	*And meanwhile*
da sempre	*forever*
rifanno	*the design*
il disegno	*is remade*
le stelle	*by the stars.*

(Recite 66 times, looking at the night sky.)

I sow thought, oh Gods, I emit thought of fire. I spread the power of Prometheus upon every planet that hosts this form of mine.

This is my challenge: to meet children, men and women who are equal to the Gods – creators of human beings and created by them.

May this alliance be holy, and wise be the power that will come from it.

May my words be not proud but just. And may men and women advance together with the Gods, who grow old and fall asleep.

May new, ancient friendly Gods awaken!

May the doors open to the Divine Eye, benevolent and beneficent, without doubts and hidden things! The only God who kept roads open and respect for Humankind, though the same has not happened with regard to him!

May words of Consciousness be pronounced.

May the purpose that is intuited by Humankind, through the race mind, through the three rivers,[18] be the anchor of the whole species and all the forms that host souls and are a bridge between the subtle and the material planes.

The smoke now rises, light and dark, toward the heavens and disperses into the ears of the Gods.

Oh Gods, messengers to still greater Divinities, wonderfully enveloped one within the other, from the infinitesimal to the only Infinite One.

You shall say that Humankind has awakened. You shall say that Humankind requires, demands its own throne.

Humankind wants to come back and be reborn in the universe. Humankind wants to be worthy again of the dominion that once was granted to it.

Now, it can.

---

[18] The "three rivers" are inherent conditionings of every human being: (i) genetics and instinct; (ii) social environment; and (iii) spiritual education.

The new race – just one humanity – rises out of the pain and suffering of the world.

And all men and women will be equal and respectful in their indispensable differences, in their unique awareness, in the use of their free will. Everyone, individually, awakened and Enlightened!

And on the journey, first the women will carry the basket, not least because the forces of growth, represented by the birch, require that women perform the rites.

May love spread with gentleness among all creatures, and a peaceful alliance be signed by all the species.

Humankind-God, through the eye of the Stellar Falcon, has found its power again.

Out of the winter, which has lasted millennia, spring has come forth, rich with buds and promises. Thought forms, ever-stronger prayers have made all this possible. A new way is being prepared for men and women filled with will, those who are free and not petty.

Those who bring knowledge and awareness together are ready to rise, to bear witness like the first Christians, with serene decisiveness, with steadfastness, constancy and consistency.

Even if the dawn for everybody seems far off, it is the duty of those who have awareness to prepare the ranks, the forces and the soldiers for the great rebirth.

The early fires in the winter night prophetically light up this world before dawn. Every village retains, in the fire, the knowledge of Prometheus, and this message echoes back from one world to the next.

Poetry? Fantasy? Drugs? Wine? Initiation?

Why do I do and write these things? And what is the key to these mixed-up words? It is not the first time I ask this, dear Reader.

Sentences without meaning, fruit of madness? What is the secret, I ask again, hidden in this strange, peculiar, absurd diary?

Actually, is there a key, a message? If not, am I therefore a poor mad hermit?

I can't remember anymore how long I've been here, among these mountains, with these few animals, the vegetable garden, the little stone house, a fireside. I can't remember and, in my silence, I can no longer tell dream from conscious thought or from automatic everyday actions. I have imagined airplanes, cars, cities ...

Are these dreams or nightmares?

Are my rites of any use?

And those rays that illuminate me from the sky at night, from a point beyond the stars: Are they real or the fruit of my sickness?

And the voices of the Gods that I transcribe: Are those intended communications, interference that I should not know of, or messages to be written thus?

And the star that only I see, that I feel is drawing near: Is it the one I dreamed about – the chariot, the bird that will take me to the stars like Krishna – or is it total fantasy?

Why then print such strange, absurd words presented in the manner you are reading? A text for Initiates only.

And you, Reader, who are you? Are you an Initiate? If so, nothing will prevent you from receiving the obscure messages.

Impossible, you say? Try it: Open these pages at random and you will always find the right sentence for you, for the circumstances, for the problem you're in ...

So what prevents you from finding all the answers inside you? All the replies are inside each human being. A man with eyes can look in vain for a light in a room, if he keeps his eyes closed. But if he looks inside, he will find rooms rich with treasures and answers.

Look at yourself, human being. Look at yourself now with gentleness and tenderness.

Through an act of creative will, you shall be the bearer of the banner of your species, the Messenger of Light to the rest of the universe: 4, 3, 2, 1.

You will be the Prometheus of millions of races!

The tree grew strong from its seed, rich with sap and dark green leaves. Amidst the grasses, at first indistinguishable, slowly it stood out.

It rose up, day after day, full of energy and the desire to live. Spring gave it a fast development and many branches and new leaves. Summer strengthened and matured it.

But when winter came, the tree lost its leaves and was left bare and alone, in the middle of the world, amidst the dead grass. And it wondered what was the reason for its solitude, why did its growth not carry on continuously from one period to the next.

"Because," replied the snow, while covering it, "you must understand what has become of you. You must make yourself aware of your strengths. This is called sleep. Waiting without leaves, bare and cold, is not useless; it is not the interruption of life. Rather, it is like dreaming, sorting the events and the knowledge of the day. It is essential to have new foundations on which to continue growing with greater strength and awareness in the spring."

Winter cuts down the weak, but strengthens and tempers those who are truly strong inside.

If your growth, oh human, has not been false, if your development has not been merely that of a seasonal shrub, winter will show it.

So, how will my death be this time?

And his, hers, yours?

In what original manner will you leave the body that hosts you? An accident, a fall, an attack, an illness?

And how shall your soul return after the winter? Which new spring will bring you back among the humans?

Just like birth, winter and death are in everyone, all seasons in every species.

May you, dear Initiate, find the will, come spring, to be reborn!

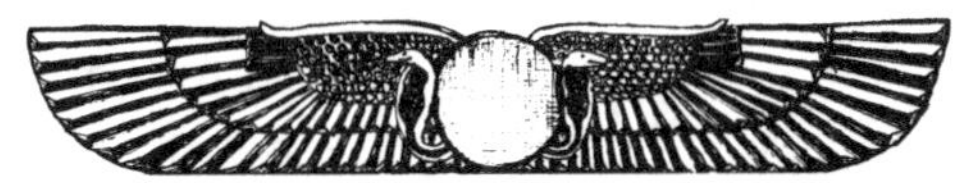

PART FIVE: FREEDOM
The Paradigm of Promise

Those who are afraid to act, unwilling to do any work, cannot be FREE.

Free are those who have nothing to lose.
Free are those who are not attached to anything but live every experience with intensity and joy.

Free are those who do not care for themselves, but for everyone, for an undefined humanity, knowing they are part of something imprecise and imperfect, which they love anyway.
Free are those who have everything to give, with generosity, because nothing holds them back.

Free are those who, like a bird, think of now with intensity and participation, of the eternal present. They live and take a dip, then fly in the sky.

When they are hungry, they seek and find, because divine providence is synchronic for every creature in the world.

Anxiety – which keeps one from sleeping, which makes one forever fear tomorrow with the sorrows and suffering and fear of today, of the present – is a trap.

And the fear of an uncertain tomorrow is paid for with the certainty of the dread of today.

How absurd all this is!

Free are those who have no taboos, who manage to overcome them and laugh at them.

Free are those who have no morals, but do nothing harmful toward others.

Free are those who fight with all their being for an ideal that will not bring them any advantages, glory or possessions, because they are so strong and so whole in the world as to have no need of them.

Free are those who fight for justice, for the things they believe in, whatever the cost.

Those who are free know how to love, and those who become free can learn to love.

Those who are free are brothers and sisters and lovers of all the earthly and the non-earthly forms. They are citizens of the world and the universe.

Those who are free respect those who are different, and they demand respect, with firmness.

Those who are free love and feel for their enemy who is mean and closed in his mind, slave to his own petty fears, but they are also ready to give him a punch on the nose!

Those who are free, SEE.

Those who are free are like the sun and the moon: mighty and great, but able to follow a stable orbit throughout eternity.

Those who are free have no need of contracts; they give their word and know how to honor it with consistency, whatever may happen.

Those who are free are not afraid of their passions and are able to recognize themselves for who and what they are. Only by recognizing themselves can they improve. Only by knowing their own limits can they truly broaden their boundaries.

And then, those who are free enjoy themselves. They are everywhere and do not waste a second of their lives.

They swim in a sense of humor and are disenchanted with the hypnotic lights of the world. They catch the agreeable and amusing and the absurd aspect of everything, even when tragic.

God – as the Great Humorist – acknowledges as great only those who are able to laugh.

Last but not least, those who are free do not fear the judgment of others, the ill words that cowards are prone to direct with relish at Initiates, whom they do not understand.

No free human being can be blackmailed. Strength lies in being free from desire and therefore unassailable, invincible.

Only those who are free become Enlightened.

Enlightenment only takes a moment, although lengthy is the preparation to convince oneself that a moment is sufficient to be the Buddha, to become Enlightened.

Alfo, I see my material dream grow with unknown strength and new laws. So what fruit did these creatures gather in times past to produce now such effects, opportunities, conditions?

Do they now want to ascend to us?

And is there a chance they might catch our Divine thoughts? That they might speak to us from their negligible will with moments of Consciousness?

Does the Game perhaps have new strength and new players? Truly, they cast their vision as far as us!

I would like to destroy the jealousy that reigns inside Humankind, which everyone has experienced.

When jealousy possesses you, what can you do?

How do you defeat this Enemy?

I remember when I was young, my Master discussed this topic. Listening to him, there were Initiates older than I, but OroCritshna, seemingly on purpose, spoke more willingly to us young ones than to the older students.

He said that thanks to the road made smooth by those who came before, those who arrive last have the duty, pursuant to their own commitment, to create a faster road for those who get stuck in habits, or who have been tested through time by his teaching.

"How many," he queried, "will still be my faithful followers when the Dark Forces turn against my teaching?"

And so he discussed jealousy.

He said that some would hinder rather than help those who arrive last, and that such pettiness was not right.

He also taught that those who are jealous are like those who favor one organ of their body and neglect the others, considering them less important. All organs must be nourished if the body is to function properly.

Then, after showing patience, OroCritshna got tired and disappointed us in order to get rid of us.

Some went away scandalized. Others, with broader minds, made their faith stronger, and became younger than us young ones.

Jealousy is possessiveness, and those who are free cannot possess anything, least of all those people or ideals they love.

The Initiate who attains Freedom will give his absolute fidelity – on every plane – to the person or principle he has chosen, the partner or purpose that has chosen him.

One who honestly makes this decision will, thereafter, consistently keep his word to his beloved and to his mission, whatever may happen.

Is this an essential part of the teaching?
Is this part of living the moment?

A Moment

Why do I fear ridicule?
Why when I go back to the village I come from,
do I at times feel a little afraid of not being "okay" in the
eyes of the country folk who laugh
behind my back?

Oh, God:
Don't let me lose awareness in this ridiculous manner.
What a sin is mine:
Being afraid of gestures of mockery is not for an Initiate!
I, who have offered to fight and hold the flag high
to defend my Master, afraid of mere words!
And yet, I remain sensitive to their dislike and liking.

I remember what my Master said on this subject. One day OroCritshna explained that the first impression we have of people may be quite correct, but it also happens that people change. Therefore, if you don't like one of your brothers, it is not right to continue thinking of him with the preconception that he cannot change and transform his way of being.

Everybody changes. Those who are Initiates have this power even more, and we have the power to recognize the possibility of their changing.

To free oneself from "sin" means freeing oneself from selfishness.

Be naive, he used to say: "It is better to be taken for a fool and to allow others the possibility of conforming to a positive thought, than to consider them cunning and let them think badly of themselves."

No human being is bad, but lack of education, presumption, weakness can be mistaken for wickedness.

Only selfishness reaches these negative heights.

How many times have I played games with my Master! How many times have I tried to send him thoughts, concentrating until I was sweating! And he, always with a smile upon his lips, pretended nothing was happening!

Other times, he would reply in a subtle, different form to my thoughts, often with a sense of humor, and always keeping me in doubt.

I understood that I should not look for proof of his powers, that this was a trap on my path: dwelling on appearances and on the polluting need for control which has led to the annihilation of civilizations.

I remember the smell of the fire and the sharp fall air nipping under the blankets pulled over our shoulders, all of us gathered together around the Master and the fire.

OroCritshna would speak, and in his calm voice he told of marvelous things, putting ideas and secrets into our young minds, a little at a time.

How many roads have opened up since then. How many doors opened wide to reveal mysterious and enticing worlds!

All of us were touched. All of us, some more than others, felt the power of his words. All the Initiates who met him were given wonderful opportunities and possibilities.

We drew cards, threw the seven stones, played drums, enacted magical games, performed rituals, dances and examinations of the future – all with the goal of finding and following and discovering our path at his side.

Yet, few have remained faithful to him.

Now, come to think about it, many hung around him like buzzards, few as his children and friends. Often, his words were used for taking something, not for understanding.

Thus, there were those who attempted to keep open the path of their awareness, but who did not have sufficient strength to carry on and do what they had sworn.

And there were those who kept hold of the ideas and the goal, yet tarried along the path and got stuck.

And there were those who betrayed.

What is required to be secret must be kept secret.

Divest yourself of every fear. Throw off the garments of your taboos. What is individual dignity but maintaining consistency without fear of ridicule?

Those who do not fear for themselves and are pure enough to understand the value of the moment lived, the eternal present, are not bound by conventions, taboos and morals, and never will be.

What do you want to hide, after all? Parts of yourself you are ashamed of? Shame of your body?

But what is shame? Is it fear of losing social ascendancy, dignity?

And what is dignity? If, as I was saying, dignity is consistency, then a person who is consistent with his own ideas is not afraid of losing consistency by performing acts that are based on the principles of his creed.

Thereafter, the opinions of others have no value, since they originate from different ideas and different goals.

Thus, those Initiates who are consistent cannot let themselves be bothered if their ideas provoke negative impressions in others.

If that happens it is because the Consciousness of those who are opposed is not sufficient. They may partially see the worthiness of the goal, but to them the idea is not important enough to make a personal sacrifice. They are afraid.

Therefore, when put to the test, those who are afraid only delude themselves, as they are neither "consistent" nor "aware." Truly, they still have deeply rooted taboos and unconscious fears.

Be afraid of my consistency? No.

To meet people full of hope in me and not let them down is a beautiful and harmonious goal.

The players in the Game of Life follow me around, free people, whose worried families and relatives throw nets and hooks. But they throw nets for me too, out of too much love for them.

What are we becoming? Continuous control produces strange effects.

The weariness of the body is compensated for by the light of the eyes, shining mirrors toward the All.

I read the eyes every day.

Identification

How difficult it is at times to distinguish the necessary from the superfluous, too much from enough.

There repeats itself the clash between sea and rocks, will and passivity, constant commitment and immobility. But the sea is stronger, the rock will be submerged, and a little at a time it will be transformed into adaptable, soft sand.

Nourish the strength that is with you, oh Initiate.

Do not refuse the effort, the difficult path,

Love the difficulties of the treacle word, tear down, start again. Be a perpetual wave. Grow and submerge everything with life.

May you be anointed of God and a bearer of *the* word.

The olive tree, sacred to Athena, was used by the great Hittite king to make an oil to anoint himself with, and con-secrating himself to Marduk, make himself invincible.[19]

---

19 Marduk was a Sumerian deity.

In Indifference, love finds an answer and the understanding of Cercops.[20]

The Divine Serpent represents death and life in nature. This is *Dharma*, the right path ...

Loving is beautiful. Bitter, instead, are the hours of slavery if loving is possessive.

In my life I have loved those who, with gentleness and joy and all of themselves, invite the beautiful, the imaginative, the renewal of every minute.

But the Enemy of everyone has noticed us and will do everything to, once again, crush humanity – crush you by destroying me.

In the middle of your ranks, when you are not on your guard, when you secretly doubt, it worms its way in and shows you the other face of Janus.[21]

Slyness and laziness *versus* ingenuousness and commitment.

I *versus* us.

The Master – who feared nothing – secretly possessed three fears. OroCritshna confided that he was greatly afraid of stupidity, superficiality, and laziness.

Yet, I know you do not abandon me, Lord, even when I am down and find it difficult to see your paternal hand in human events.

____

[20] Cercops was an early Greek poet and author of *The Descent to Hades*.
[21] Janus was a Roman god who marked transitions and had two faces: one to see the past and one to see the future.

Rebellion

Today, I have not gone out. It is raining. Water finds all the right roads to descend from the sky upon the earth. It runs down the roof, down the windows of the house. Only the leaves and the branches are moving. The birds are shut up in their feathers.

Solitude is sweet with the purifying rain.

Oh beneficial rain, tear away from the sky and the air the sicknesses that human beings have sown in so many years of STUPIDITY.

I refer to the corrupt, utter moral filth of certain dealers, or executors of power.

I address myself to those incompetents who make use of a show of force in the form of a beret, badge or uniform and behind which they hide their pettiness, their nothingness, in order to abuse the rights of humanity.

Puffed up with their hubris, convinced they represent forces that render them untouchable, barricaded behind their gibbering, presumptuous ignorance, with insane pleasure they normally, regularly, take advantage in exercising their apparent power, which in reality is mean-minded violence.

Mad impotent beings, lost among the nightmares and the bitter ghosts of their contorted minds, they abuse the weak, the pure, the naive, the trusting, the friend, the simple, the honest man.

All Humankind – every one of us – will recognize ourselves in one of these opposing ranks.

But in this New Paradigm there shall prevail New Human Beings who cannot be bribed, nor beaten, nor humiliated, nor stripped, because they have nothing to hide except what others want to see hidden, nothing to humiliate because they are beyond morality and conventions, nothing to be robbed of because they possess what cannot be taken from them – themselves, nothing to beat down because they have the strength of their ideas.

The Enlightened Human Beings, steady in their faith, consistently and indifferently overcome every obstacle.

They are Being.
They are Truth.

Zela, they have discovered that the fruit of action is awareness in action. Now, with the cost of Freedom and the favor of Free Will, they can access ever greater parts of the magical formula leading up to us. I admire so much their bravery!

Still, the wall of consistency and continuity defended by the forces of laziness and weariness separates them from the Door. Some try and I feel that their presumption may be, in reality, their courageous right.

Yes, some Enlightened Ones catch our thoughts, Zela. Their glances dare – in Being and in Truth – to find forces able to equal us.

Fortunately, the forces of chance are subjugated by Synchronicity. But darker forces now have noticed them and will try again to annihilate them.

Let us hear your thoughts on the matter ...

Part Six: Zela
Meditative Poetry

The season changes.
The sky is black in the orient.
In the air already you sense
a quiver of love ...

I am Passion. I am a love concentrated and compressed, kept hidden by gestures and gentle smiles. I greet, watch, caress with my eyes your scented skin, your fingers, your glances, your gestures, your words well hidden by your good manners.

I feel your thoughts exploding, passionate and full of desire and longing for love.

I pretend I do not notice. I watch.

I share in your feelings without upsetting your existence.

I secretly know every sweetness of your body, all the beauty and delicateness mixed together in time, your silences, our silences, and the walls that divide us in distant houses.

Every "I" comprises a box ready to comprise another box. Everything completes itself, in thoughts and desires.

But beauty and mutual attraction are not enough to bring us close: it takes more, much more.

The fleeting moment of our meeting, full of honey and sweet thoughts and caresses, is often the memory of another time, of another life. An existence in a far away epoch recalled from beyond the river of time, of the centuries. Memories of things lived, languor, disappointed hopes, unfinished meetings, and uncompleted love.

Ah, if only you could, like me, remember.

I have met you clad in different costumes, with features barely resembling your present ones. I have loved you in moments and manners that are lost to you now.

You swore eternal love to me, and now that the years have brought us close, you can't recognize me! Even this is divine humor ...

The eternal, the oath, the passion, a few years later are nothing but dim, yellowed memories.

I clearly recall how we met, how we loved one another. I remember details, epochs, the name of your parents, your name that I would gently whisper, and listening to my name sighed and repeated by you in my ear.

Wife or sweet lover, how can you meet my glance and not remember?

How can you remain close to me without a shiver, a faint flash of memory that you take for a figment of your imagination, or a true memory of the intensity of the passion that devoured us? Can you not fall in love with me again?

I see floating and flowing by, on the water of time, all the dear objects that belonged to you, that belonged to us.

I see between the rocks, in pools of water, the face that you had then, and the smiling or harsh faces of friends and enemies.

I remember our conversations and promises so much more intensely than those I fixed in my memory today, words and eternal oaths that occupy the space of one night.

Why do you think I am so sweet?

We only brushed one another with a glance, but an intense red and yellow wave of feelings crossed the space between us.

The Light and the Dark draw us close. The memories are inside of me only. You don't even remember your name.

I, perhaps, don't recognize your name in this life now. Not because I live in memories, but because a name has no importance except when it is whispered.

Maya

Something that glitters deludes you,
and you run and look because you are confused.
It is only a shiny bit of broken pottery,
useless and destroyed.

Time flies by and is lacking.
You wait at the mysterious opening,
wide-eyed,
pondering the illusion ...

Evening Star

Oh, first star of the evening,
I am not abandonment but solitude.
Will you come with me?

Travelling is a school. The camp is set up in the wood, and the beach is quite near.

The music sews the souls of those present. It weaves around the fire fanciful and fascinating threads.

The dogs follow my journey. Everywhere, beings take a body in one of these hospitable creatures. The little people participate, in secret, full of joy and a vibrant lust for life. Little animals listen to guitars and drums in fascination.

I like to experience such enfoldments, a thousand involutions. To fly over ancient temples and ragged rocks, to swim beneath the waves, to run through the rustling and fragrant grass of the savannah.

Free from form, I am the atom of the world, the flower, the shell, the insect on a gigantic planet ...

Colors upon colors explode from the songs and the rhythms, volcanic eruptions from the depths of the self.

Oh you, kind wanderer – you, who give shelter to the stranger and the destitute, you who feed those starving for life – be reborn to the beautiful and the great, from the pain of the "I" for the other "I-Me's."

The little boat with sails made from carrier bags and lit with hollowed out oranges travels safe, carrying my message to the sea.

It is as far as the horizon, yet it is near since it lives on imagination, pirates, magical signs.

Like the first star of the evening.

Three Times

Three times, three young girls
listened to the message
and answered "yes."

Three genies of the earth
smiled dancing, clapping,
clapping their hands.

Three trees in the wind waved leafy branches
and a ray of sunshine
was clipped several times.

Three times an ant
climbed up and down the rose
milking green aphids.

Three times from the house
a smile burst from the children
and the ball bounced higher and higher.

Three times the restless bird
left the safe nest
and the eggs became cold.

Three times the dog barked at the hens
and the astrologer raced
to anxiously put on paper his intuition.

Three times
the bell chimed
and I woke up.

Joy

Thoughts full of joy color every corner, every shadowed place with lively light. In the midst of cheerful, serene creatures, eyes become bright.

Gestures, laughs and games rejuvenate – like a gymnasium of life – every atrophied muscle of the face: 4, 3, 4, 4.

And laugh, laugh, you learn by laughing a hundred times better and more. Look with joy, play games, joke in order to know, to understand.

Love passes through games and joy.

Joy, may you give meaning to everything, to everything more, more everything.

I know the ink in this pen has been forever destined to spread itself in words on these pages. And I know that it can run out and the pen be refilled ... changed.

I know how the black clouds close in and how the watchful eye of power scrutinizes me, suspicious and threatening.

Joy, may you give meaning to everything.

Fear

A little fear
in a little room
seems,
to a little man,
a big fear
that fills the room.

Directions

If your advice is sought, don't feel superior for having been asked.

Give the direction, not the address.

Allow others to navigate their own path and they will be more apt to accept your advice.

They will understand if they want to understand.

Reply "yes" to whoever seeks yes; reply "no" to whoever wants no.

Rightly reply to those who rightly ask.

Partial Success

I asked, "Is there total Enlightenment or only partial flashes of enlightened Consciousness?"

He replied, "There is total Enlightenment and it is achievable even in this life."

The moments, the flashes of Enlightenment that give life a reason and a purpose, are the prelude, the dawn before the sunrise.

They are the dawning.

Without these partial flashes of Enlightenment one could never endure total solar Enlightenment.

Remember: God put the matches in your hand but you must light them.

Mutiny

I dream of sails, pale sails against similar pale backgrounds, upon seas identical to nothingness, alike in color, in the clouds, in the seashells.

Mute mirrors to questions, tired eyes forever the same, hands that wear out the years, the words, the opportunities. Firm bodies become heavy, and still more time, more words, more opportunities are lost.

Living like this, dying like this, suffering like this ... always waiting for something, for someone, for oneself.

Food, sleep, sex, work, fears, fantasies, disappointments, weariness. Laziness, tiredness, desire, love.

And consistency? And one's given word? And the use of one's talents for their worth?

Love opposed to power, power that is a lack of love.

Your I, with which you carefully avoid talking, tells you uncomfortable, annoying things, that fortunately only you know. And you are offered the chance to break the black circle in which you are condemned.

You ditch everything, you are yourself.

Now, what do you do?

The Latest Life

Time like a wave – now slow, now voracious of shores, vulnerable things – crashes and creates an undertow.

Meanwhile, the sun has set, and pen and paper mingle in the blue darkness of written words.

In this current time, in the space of miles and geography, I know that you act, talk, and live, even if far away from me.

But where? With whom?

A star has lit up the sky. How many of us are watching the same star, the same sea right now?

In the remains of the silence, how many generations have listened to these eternal sounds?

Later, darkness further veils my words and creates red reflections on the horizon of this day, ablaze and gone forever upon a flat shelf of black clouds.

Never again this day, but maybe a ghost in my memory or writing. I do not know if I shall ever read again these sentences which I offer to whomever, to who may be, to the others in time, who come and then disappear.

The one you would want isn't here ... and if he were here you wouldn't want him.

What sense does this make, writing in the dark?

Ever more indefinite outlines reunite me with an eternity of symbols, with the Great Mother from whom I arose and to whom I shall return, a raindrop in the ocean.

Is it not odd that "mare" is "madre" without a "d"?[22]

How many more times – from life to life – must I hold these memories within me?

And is it my duty to tell others? To unveil, reveal, make understand, spark the imagination, confuse, make think?

Solitude of Consciousness, whose diversity I jealously preserve, do you offer a defense against the present life, so different than the last?

Will I, like Ulysses, see my Ithaca again?

---

[22] In Italian, *mare* is the sea, and *madre* means mother.

Thoughts of a Girl

Girl with the beautiful eyes
smile at me
showing perfect teeth
from soft, full lips.
Turn me on, girl,
with glances and little tosses of your head.

You stroke your hair, girl,
and thoughts escape
that you would never speak
with your soft lips
that show perfect teeth ...

Someone: A Moment

Sweetest Thing: Renunciation is not love. The moment
is also:
a sweet whisper
a caress in the night
breath in the ear
smell of young skin
warmth of a hand on a cold shoulder
opening your eyes to find a smile welcoming you
a kiss between dream and not dream
a taste of sleep.

Grotto on the Sea

Alone, amid so many who love me, who hazily intuit who I am, who trust me now.

Future cities and civilizations, like a tide coming in and going out, cover the stones with spirit and collapse back upon themselves.

I prefer the present, sung by sweet voices charged with feelings, sung out of tune or in melodious voices, yet joined now in awareness in this brief moment.

It is teaching, it is wandering, it is school and it is life. Dreaming and sighing.

By the light of the torch, in the dark, I sense monsters and huge, slow, silent leviathans moving in the abyss.

Will they come up to the grotto tonight, under the quarter moon?

What is it that ruffles this sea, observing me from the darkness down there?

What mysteries, Humankind, on this contested planet of yours?

And the moon, a slice of moon, is up above me, between opposing clouds, dark and swift.

The sea has changed its voice, it makes us shiver, and the blackness of the waves pours toward Me-Us.

I have already died more than once in the sea.

I lift my head, suddenly, remembering sounds that re-echo from it – the Deep – the eternal element that is death and life.

A huge halo now surrounds Selene. The shadows move soundlessly, coiled low like mysterious serpents, and so many stars draw the heavens.

Will the gully of this steep mount close in upon me? How long has it been waiting for me?

This salty smell, this water, will it yet again slip over my bones? I will disappear and no one will know ... a myth among myths, story bait for winter evenings, to tingle spines around the fire.

The foam spreads over the sand, and bombardments of waves that seem longer and longer cut off paths, while infinite reflections of the moon are born upon the sinuous sea.

I can almost see with that sliver of moon, and I now catch a glimpse of the words lived as intense, multiform moments just a while ago.

I am in the MOMENT.

I am the Self and the All, in Truth.

I am fish, little animals hiding. I am the others who are far away, and I am even in you.

The All am I, the everywhere, as long as the moment pervades me.

Let's go. Someone, still, needs you.

There is always, always, for everyone, secretly, someone who is waiting.

Every being is lonely and afraid of itself. Is it this fear that distinguishes the one from the All? What establishes the boundaries of the I?

A breath of wind, a fresh rustling, a sigh of the Self distinguishes the form of the human being, measuring it in the "buts" and the "maybes."

Self-doubt: consistent prey that offers itself to the fisherman. No stone is the same as another and on the sand there are millions upon millions of stones. Human beings. Crystals.

Flickering thoughts hanging over the bridge of memories, while the words lose their meaning, mislay their forms, become living organisms, magical fruit of action and nexus of creation. I am thinking.

A great rock in the shape of a dog lays its muzzle into the sea. Little extinct seashells, with no current history, lie down with their tummies in the air, trying in vain to remember who they have been.

When the sea speaks, the dunes are asleep and make not the tiniest sound.

Every drawing traced by finger on the sand will stay more eternal than the pyramids. The centuries will bow down to address and adore every little grain.

Tonight, perhaps a tiny crab will cross the entire infinite beach. Perhaps it will clamber over the seashells and the small dunes. Perhaps the sea will open to let it pass, in silence. Perhaps it will find a treasure and not know what to do with it.

It certainly won't find food, no nourishment, on the eternal beach.

Tomorrow, I will give it crumbs. I will place them down over there ... at the bottom of the hollow ... a thousand little crab steps beyond ...

The crab will find the crumbs if it knows how to seek. It may lose its way, but then find the road again.

And it will die all the times that it needs to.

Once a stone decided to be more beautiful than the others. It turned to the sea and asked for help to model itself.

During what was, for it, a short period of time, the stone had been satisfied. But for Humankind, just out of the caves, it was a long enough span to create civilizations and desire collections.

The stone, so very beautiful, was boasting about itself and tumbling around on the sand by complaisant waves. Radiant among the other stones, admired by millions of its companions, happy, it was picked up by a collector and isolated in a glass case, far from its own kind.

What a joke!

Beautiful beyond comparison loses its preeminence and becomes commonplace when surrounded by other beauties. And if a person sees only beautiful things for too long, he will seek and recognize himself thenceforth only in the wonderful.

Without opposites nothing has value, and the price of what is rare only makes desire increase ...

The thoughts of the creatures on the beach weave arabesques and colored embroideries in forms and actions of continuous growth.

Spirit exercises its muscles in the dialogue and in the exchanges. The words communicate and broaden the Me in the Us.

My sense of the nothingness plays among the shadows of the little ravines, in the rocks. Smell of spray and of lively sea that polishes its own collection of strange stones.

With the hours, the tide has come in and gone out. A fine sparkling mist rises from the foam and glazes the beach, immediately disappearing.

Torn, green and black, yellowed seaweeds are life's tribute to the Mother.

Who lives here? What creatures have their civilization in the rocks?

Little scorpions lead their silent existence among the stones and the rosemary, as guardians to the deep voice of the sea: "If I take a stone in my hand, I awaken its soul."

Every stone awaits the hand that will free it from the nothingness and give it self-awareness.

The crab has reached my crumbs.

Oracle

Dream sustained with eyes closed
Binds gestures to reality
Caresses without words
Rare secret thoughts
All slowed down and lived outside of Time

PART SEVEN: ALFO
Possible Conclusions

After meditating at length one night, the Time Monk Vadusfadam pens a piece for his followers, which I relate here as follows:

WARNING:

The Forces of Enlightenment are becoming denser, but the Enemies of Humankind are aware of this foreshadowing and will react with every means available.

The army of the New Human Being is not yet ready.

The moon is punctual in drawing to an important phase, and the planets have aligned the four ancient, allied Forces of Humankind, which will flow through me.

The risk for me is great, but lost time may be recovered with the aid of past players and new recruits.

Current Initiates are assessed based on their consistency. All can reach the summit by aiming for the bulls-eye and committing total presence and will to the optimal end.
Soon, the state of your metamorphosis will be apparent.

May you be united, clear, and constant.
It will be the little, seemingly negligible challenges that will yield the principal elements for transformation.
You will be Buddhas – innovators of the world – if you are consistent and truly seek to answer the questions the Game poses along the way.

Fear of ridicule? You are its slave and you will be freed.
Fear of others? You will be the strength of others.
Fear of pain? You will have bliss and nothing will be able to impair the power of the Free Human.
And the same for every other fear.

The Game proceeds round by round, and those who understand the rules will receive multiple opportunities to reach the goal.
Every Initiate has something essential to offer others. You will not reach Enlightenment if you fail to provide for others first. Use your free will to grow not in habit but in continuous renewal and evolution.
The tests are precisely designed for every single player – that much the Synchronic Forces allow me.

Enjoy yourselves and stay alert! Everything is a Sign.
Five times the stars, three times the triangles, three circles and the fifth and sixth word.

May each Initiate become an active organizer, courageous and confident of the power he or she has inside.

What does this message mean?
Three hundred and thirty-three (333) words?

His friends, the few, are convinced that in his diary and other writings, Vadusfadam has surely encoded and transmitted magical formulas.

He is either an alchemist of the word in contact with tremendous forces ... or a madman.

The seed planted by Master OroCritshna grew inside Vadusfadam, and he has now sown the seed on earth through a new army of Initiates.

Will the seed mature into a glorious tree of life?
Or not?

Possible Endings

OPTION 1:

One evening, while Vadusfadam was talking with a few young Initiates, a bright light came from the heavens and illuminated him. He was transformed into OroCritshna, rose up into the light, and reached the stars.
Humankind was liberated.

But is this a decent ending?
Let's take a look at another one ...

OPTION 2:

Vadusfadam grew old and remained wise. He transmitted many teachings to his children, for the whole world. He died in curious circumstances, alone, and still no one knows where his body is to be found.
He is in everyone.

And some more possibilities:

OPTION 3:

While Vadusfadam was talking, he suddenly stopped and fell silent. He shouted "NOW!" and drew in the air with a few gestures, in front of a standing stone – a Door.
His shape in the air shone and pulsated. He passed to the other side of the portal, then poked his head out of the Nothingness and called some of his followers.
They chose to follow him with joy. One by one, they entered into the Nothingness trembling with anticipation and singing. Some, too "thick," did not manage to pass. They found solid stone and pushed to no avail.
Then the Door disappeared in a great burst of laughter that echoed for a long time from the rocks.

OPTION 4:

Vadusfadam was locked up in an asylum where he died, giggling away.

OPTION 5:

Then there came a great white bird, upon which Vadusfadam mounted like a horse. At the break of dawn, he disappeared toward the sun, after saying goodbye and kissing all the Initiates, who were Enlightened.

OPTION 6:

They came to arrest him because he created trouble with his ideas. They accused Vadusfadam of many crimes and flung him into prison. They built up evidence against him to destroy his philosophy.
They succeeded.

OPTION 7:

And then the sea opened, and Vadusfadam slowly began to descend toward the center of the earth, between walls of water that quickly became a tunnel. One Initiate went with him.
No one saw them again upon this world.

OPTION 8:

After lengthy meditation, Vadusfadam decided it was not yet time to reveal to Humankind what OroCritshna had taught him. His life had been spent in vain, as his disciples were too slow, too heavy, too bound to fly.
Thus, he recanted everything and said, "It was all a joke, guys."
He lived an almost normal life, until he died.

OPTION 9:

Not having succeeded in realizing the purpose of his coming and his time having elapsed, Vadusfadam paid the gambling debt – according to the Law – with his material life and with suffering.
Then he committed suicide.

OPTION 10:

He said that with the power of Love, he would take on with consistency the ills of the world. He then channeled the impulse of Love, thereby providing one last lesson to his adepts.
Vadusfadam died of cancer a few months later.

OPTION 11:

The army of Initiates, along with Vadusfadam, built a new society comprised of many small Cities of Light all over the world.
It was thus that the New Era began.

OPTION 12:

Vadusfadam disappeared into thin air, all of a sudden. No one remembered anything.
Will he try again in a few centuries?

OPTION 13:

Vadusfadam's disciples did not understand a thing he had said, and therefore founded a new religion in his name.
He died of a heart attack.

Which is your preferred ending?
And which is the likely outcome?
You, who are reading in another time, will remember what historically happened.

Yet, time is one of the great illusions.
There exists a cornucopia of potential endings ...

In this round of the Game, the conclusion depends solely upon *your* actions ...
On the Light that is within *you* ...
And on what *you* choose to do with *your* free will: 6, 4, 3, 3.

ABOUT THE AUTHOR

OBERTO *"Falco"* AIRAUDI

Oberto Airaudi is Damanhur's Spiritual Guide. His teachings encourage the awakening of the inner master through study, experimentation, overcoming dogmatic attitudes, and the complete expression of individual potential.

Born in 1950 in Balangero, Italy (near Turin), Mr. Airaudi is a philosopher, healer, writer, and painter. He is constantly involved in research into cutting-edge therapeutic applications, the arts and new sciences. In accordance with the Damanhurian custom of being called by animal names, Mr. Airaudi also uses the name of "Falco" (Falcon).

He chose this name to honor Horus, symbol of the divine principle to be awakened inside every human being and the cosmic God of the New Millennium.

From a very early age, Falco manifested a clear spiritual vision and the gift of healing. He committed to develop these gifts through constant and exacting experimentation, outside of traditional academic institutions. His spiritual and personal growth continued over the years via incessant studies, journeys of research, the awakening of his memories, the development of artistic skills, and the rediscovery of ancient knowledge.

In 1975, Falco founded the Horus Center in Turin. It was the first seed of a Mystery School and a community, and from its activities the Federation of Damanhur developed.

Damanhur was born to realize the dream of a society based on optimism and the idea that human beings can be the masters of their own destiny, without having to depend on other forces outside themselves. Indeed, the basis of Falco's vision is the belief that every human being participates, through conscious interactions with others, to awaken a divine nature within themselves. As a result, Damanhur is a society in constant evolution and transformation, based on the exaltation of diversity. Its social, political, and philosophical systems are always in flux.

Falco is a remarkably reserved person, and he has no decision-making role within the political or social structure of Damanhur, which is directed by elected bodies. If asked, he is always available to cooperate with the Federation's Guides, who are elected by the citizens.

About Damanhur

Founded in 1975, the Federation of Damanhur is an Italian eco-society based upon ethical and spiritual values. Damanhur has about 1,000 citizens and extends over 500 hectares of land throughout the Valchiusella region, at the foothills of the Piedmont Alps.

Damanhur is approximately 90% self-sustainable, with more than 80 businesses that foster agricultural and economic independence. Damanhur has a Constitution, complementary currency system, daily newspaper, art studios, centers for research and practice of medicine and science, open university, and education for children from elementary through middle school.

Damanhur promotes a culture of peace and equitable development through solidarity, volunteerism, respect for the environment, art, and social and political engagements. Courses and events are open to the public year round, and it is possible to visit for short periods as well as longer stays for study, vacation, or regeneration.

Damanhur's Temples of Humankind – often called the "Eighth Wonder of the World" – comprise an extraordinary underground network of chapels dedicated to the reawakening of the divine essence in every human being. The art studios that contributed to the stained glass, mosaics, and frescoes in the Temples are located at Damanhur Crea, a center for innovation, wellness, and research, which is open to the public every day of the year.

Damanhur operates additional centers in Italy, Europe, Japan, and the United States. Damanhur also collaborates with other international organizations engaged in the social, civic, and spiritual development of the planet.

Damanhur has received world-wide recognition for its innovative and inspiring approach to life. Since 1988, Damanhur has been a member of the Global Eco-Villages Network, and in 2005 it received a United Nations sustainability award. In 2007, *EnlightenNext* magazine voted Damanhur the most evolved community on earth.

Please visit the Damanhur website for additional information and directions on how to visit the community.

www.Damanhur.org

About the Publisher

The Truth

The founders of The Oracle Institute are gravely concerned that the greatest crisis facing humanity is the resurgence of religious intolerance perpetrated in the name of God. We chose the Pentacle as our icon because, to us, this symbol represents the emerging spiritual unification of the five primary religions: Hinduism, Judaism, Buddhism, Christianity, and Islam. We believe the time has come for humanity to shed archaic belief systems and prepare for the next phase of our collective spiritual evolution.

The Love

The Oracle Institute promotes a process of soul growth which includes study, worship, meditation, and good works through application of the Golden Rule: the "Eleventh Commandment" brought by Jesus. When we earnestly strive to perfect ourselves, practice compassion toward others, and assume responsibility for the health of our planet, we help birth a new spiritual paradigm.

The Light

Many people are now ready to manifest "heaven on earth" – the prophesied era of abundance, peace, and harmony foretold by the prophets of every religion and the elders of every indigenous wisdom culture. To that end, The Oracle Institute offers interfaith books, spirituality classes, civics seminars, health and mindfulness programs, and holistic products designed to foster the quest for spiritual enlightenment.

We Invite You to Join Us on Our Journey of

TRUTH, LOVE, and LIGHT

Donations may be made to:

THE ORACLE INSTITUTE
A 501(c)(3) Educational Charity

*An Advocate for Enlightenment and
A Vanguard for Spiritual Evolution*

1990 Battlefield Drive
Independence, Virginia 24348
www.TheOracleInstitute.org

All donations and proceeds from our books and classes are used to further our educational mission and to build the Peace Pentagon, an interfaith and social justice center in Independence, Virginia.

9 781937 465056